HOME OF THE BRAVE

HOME OF THE BRAVE

CONTEMPORARY AMERICAN IMMIGRANTS

MARY MOTLEY KALERGIS

E. P. DUTTON NEW YORK

OTHER BOOKS BY MARY MOTLEY KALERGIS

Mother: A Collective Portrait

Giving Birth

Copyright © 1989 by Mary Motley Kalergis
Foreword copyright © 1989 by Cornell Capa
All rights reserved. Printed in Portugal

No part of this publication may be reproduced or transmitted
in any form or by any means, electronic or mechanical, including
photocopy, recording, or any information storage and retrieval
system now known or to be invented, without permission in writing
from the publisher, except by a reviewer who wishes to quote
brief passages in connection with a review written for inclusion
in a magazine, newspaper, or broadcast.

Published in the United States by E. P. Dutton,
a division of Penguin Books USA Inc.,
2 Park Avenue, New York, N.Y. 10016.

Published simultaneously in Canada
by Fitzhenry and Whiteside, Limited, Toronto.

Library of Congress Cataloging-in-Publication Data

Home of the brave: contemporary American immigrants
[compiled by] Mary Motley Kalergis.—1st ed.
p.   cm.
ISBN 0-525-24762-9
1. Immigrants—United States—Interviews. 2. United States—
Emigration and immigration. I. Kalergis, Mary Motley.
JV6455.5.H66   1989
325.73—dc19   88-27316
                             CIP

Designed by Nancy Etheredge

10 9 8 7 6 5 4 3 2 1

First Edition

To my beloved husband,
David,
my hero and greatest fan.

Acknowledgments

I'd like to give special thanks to certain people whose enthusiasm and support helped this idea become a reality: Margaret and Walt Olin, for typing what I needed when I needed it; Crawford Sherman for giving me access to the Remington Hotel in Houston; Tottie Mitchell, for being my California tour guide; Alice Kaknes, for making the Boston trip happen; and all my students at ICP in New York City for their introductions and ideas. I feel especially fortunate to have the tender loving care of my editor, Meg Blackstone, and my agent, Susan Protter.

Introduction

Immigration is an act of courage and determination. *Home of the Brave* celebrates that optimistic pioneering spirit which holds the United States together as a nation. This collection of photographs and interviews is a portrait of America as seen in the faces and heard through the voices of its immigrants. It focuses on the character of these individuals who come from more than forty countries and live in all parts of the United States.

We are a nation of nations. Most Americans come from families who emigrated from other parts of the world. People who have made the choice to come to America have a heightened sense of this country's strengths and weaknesses because they have their original culture and tradi-tions for comparisons. As one immigrant told me, "You don't really appreciate and understand your values until you've lost everything and have to rebuild your life."

This country attracts people who are ambitious and believe in their ability to control their destinies. The political refugees who come here because their lives are threatened in their home-land share the same survivalist determination as the ambitious entrepreneur who comes here to improve his life. These are the ones who will not stay behind and accept the status quo. Freedom and opportunity are their most frequently ex-pressed desires, although not all have realized their dreams. They are living history and an im-portant part of our national character.

Foreword

Some fifty years ago, a ship carrying a young, just-graduated immigrant boy from Budapest approached the tip of Manhattan and passed the Statue of Liberty, which was barely visible through the early morning fog. The harbor bells were clanging. Today, I can still feel the excitement of that magic moment of having arrived in my new world.

Looking at the photographs and reading the stories for Mary Motley Kalergis' new book, *Home of the Brave*, brought back such memories and has rung the bells of that misty arrival in my ears once again.

Now, as the founding director of the International Center of Photography, I have both relived my own story and volunteered this introduction to her book. Here goes the current and relevant chapter in the story of this particular immigrant:

Some years after the founding of ICP in 1974, a young photographer with a radiant smile and some good prints named Mary Kalergis appeared at my doorstep. She attended our lecture series and then began teaching a course at the center. One day she visited my office with her newborn baby and the material for her forthcoming first book.

We exhibited prints at the launching of her book, and she gave a lecture on the subject, one very close to her heart, *Giving Birth*. Not too long thereafter, she published her second book, *Mother: A Collective Portrait*.

She recently appeared with a brand-new baby, Natasha, and a new body of work entitled *Home of the Brave*, portraits and interviews with first-generation immigrants that reflect so clearly her integrity and living philosophy: a receptive respect for all the people she encounters.

Mary's books now form a trilogy directly connected to her life—giving birth, a cognizance of what motherhood is all about, and her latest, a personal understanding of her country. *Home of the Brave* is a literary and visual exploration of immigrants and the process of their becoming Americans. It is a serious and honest book. Mary's images and interviews are revealing and provide insights that are important for all Americans, those who arrived a long time ago and others, whose recent experiences provide an undistorted image in the mirror of her camera—a view of contemporary American life.

My fifty years in America, my development in photography, my meeting Mary Motley Kalergis, and her development during this past decade are interwoven with ICP. Altogether they form another chapter of the immigrant story—mine added to the others. I am honored to have been included.

HOME OF THE BRAVE

Abdulah Sidiqui

I had to leave my home country of Afghanistan in 1980 when the Soviet Union invaded. I took my family to Pakistan believing that Russia wouldn't be able to complete a Communist revolution and we would be able to return to our home. I was able to better help the resistance by organizing outside of the country. For five and one-half years I worked full-time out of Pakistan helping my countrymen fight the Communists. Eventually I realized that the struggle would continue much longer, and I became worried about the education of my children. Over the years the Soviets killed all the intellectuals in my country. Teachers, doctors, lawyers, and engineers are all gone; therefore, I think I can help Afghanistan the most by getting my children a good education so one day they can go back and help rebuild my country.

My children are the main reason that we are here. I believe they will have the opportunity to choose any career they want. It's not hard for them to get a job after school because they are good children and willing to work. It's harder for me because I know I can't practice law here. I would like to do accounting, but I have to learn about computers. It is lonely for my wife because our neighbors are gone to work or are very old and never go out of the house. You never see people outside so much here. They are either in their car or inside watching TV. Even shopping for food is so hard because we don't recognize a lot of the fresh produce and it's hard to read the labels. It's hardest for my wife. She can't answer the phone or the door. I'm studying English now at the community college so I can then study computers. You've really got to speak English to get by in this country. There are so many changes to get used to. Just wearing pants is a big adjustment. We have to get used to making an appointment to go see someone. Americans are always so busy.

One of my main goals here is to let the people in America know of the crimes of the Soviet Union. They kill all the finest people when they come into a country. They destroy the entire culture that is very old and of great value. It is a terrible thing, and the world should know about the Communists. Americans should teach their children in the schools to have more patriotism. The future belongs to the children, and they must put their money into American products and not send the money out of the country. Americans have to think more about their own country as a whole and less about their individual comfort.

Lech Bledowski

I was surprised how hard it is to get a job here so I can support my family. I knew I would not be able to be a lawyer right away because we have Roman law in Poland as opposed to the common law system you have in the United States. I was willing to take any job to feed my wife and three children, but it is impossible to live on minimum wage, even when we both work. Here in Tidewater, five dollars an hour is considered good pay—but it's not nearly enough to get out of poverty. It is hard on a man when he can't support his family. I hope when I've been here five years and get my citizenship, I can get a job doing legal work and translation for immigrants and refugees. Right now my future is a big question mark. It's really a problem to have no recommendations. It helps to have connections. We are totally unconnected. All I have is my résumé and my willingness to work. I knew the streets weren't paved with gold here, but I still was not prepared for how difficult it would be to give my family food and shelter. I don't like taking food stamps. I did not come here to live on charity. I was a lawyer in my country for twelve years before I came here, so I was used to a certain standard of living and place in the community. I want to make a life for my family here similar to what I left behind. I didn't come here to be a millionaire, I emigrated because the Communists made me unwelcome in Poland.

There is a lot to get used to when you immigrate. For example, the casualness of friendships is very different than in Eastern Europe. Here people are very friendly, but they don't really take much responsiblity in their relationships. Americans are not nearly so interested in politics as Europeans because for the most part they have comfortable lives. I hope that one day my family will be comfortable too. I truly believe that a hardworking person has a chance to make a good life for himself, but you have to be able to sell yourself here. No matter how impressive your experience may be, if you don't have the skills to go out in the world and promote yourself, you don't have as much of a chance as the person who can really market himself. This is not easy for me or my wife, even though we have many years of professional experience in Poland. We have to learn to be more American and sell ourselves. It's hard to have a lot of confidence if your English is not so good, but what can I do but believe in myself? This is my life, I can't give up.

Now that I've been here four years, I have a much more realistic view of democracy. I always had a romantic idea about the system when I was behind the Iron Curtain. The pluses are very real, but so are the minuses. Even knowing the weaknesses firsthand, I would not presume to change it. In the long run it works better than anything else civilization has been able to devise so far. I'm free to fail here, but I'm also free to succeed, and I believe I ultimately will.

Anna Bledowski

My husband spent three months in prison because of his work in the Solidarity movement. His allegiance is to Poland, not the Russians, so the Communists made sure he couldn't get a job after he got out of jail. My allegiance is to my family. We really had no choice but to emigrate. We are political refugees.

When we first immigrated to the United States from Poland, I spoke no English, so it was very hard to get a job here in my profession as a physical therapist. It was even more impossible for my husband to get work as a lawyer.

I got a job housekeeping and my husband cleaned instruments in a hospital. We really miss our careers and it will take a long time before I know English well enough to study anatomy and medicine so I can get my license. Physical therapy here is treated with less respect than in Poland. I never heard about sex massage and all that foolishness they have here. In my country I worked alongside doctors in hospitals and had a lot of responsibilities. It is hard for a professional person to lose their career along with their language and culture. We left Tacoma, Washington, to come to Virginia for my husband to study on scholarship. He is looking for a job but it is not easy. We have to leave student housing because he graduates, but we have no money to move and no job to go to. Two of my children are still too young to go to school, and I can't afford a baby-sitter so I can work. It's really a very hard time in this country the first five years or so when you are learning the language. My older daughter has the easiest time.

She learns to become an American quickly because she is in school all day. I try not to feel sad, but it's an effort not to be discouraged. I think the more established you are in your country, the harder it is to relocate. We knew it would not be easy, but you can't really be prepared for what it feels like to be on the outside looking in.

My son has been very sick and I've been very frustrated with the medical care here. The doctors never listen to me—it's just "here's the medicine, now good-bye." In Poland, doctors respect mothers, since they know what is usual and what is unusual for their children. Here I am treated like I don't have good sense. When my baby daughter was born last year, they sent me home after one day. The mother gets no time to rest. Medicine is too much about making money and not enough about patient care.

It's strange for me to be home alone with the children all day. My husband has to use his car for work, and we can't afford two. There is no bus service near the apartment where we live and there's really nowhere to walk to—no public park or town square like in Europe. It's almost like being in prison. This town has no center, just mile after mile of apartments and gas stations. There aren't even any sidewalks. Everything is so far apart, you've got to have a car to do much of anything. Being so isolated is bad for your nerves. I don't want to complain. I'm just telling the truth about the first few years of immigrating. It is not easy to start a new life.

Hyon Ju Scotton

Even as a little girl in Korea, I was always aware of the United States. Its presence is felt everywhere in my country. I got a job at a U.S. Army officers' club as a waitress so I could learn to speak good English. You could get a better job if you speak English. I met my American husband there. I didn't let my parents know I was working there or going out with an American, because I knew they wouldn't like it. It was a big decision whether I should leave my country for a man. I came to America with him before we got married to see if I could adjust. I must admit that when we drove across this country, it was not like my dream. The middle of the country seems boring and everyone looked at me like I was strange. I really like the West Coast though; it is more like my country, but people here seem to be always in a hurry and impatient. I've been here a little over two years now. At first I felt so shy to be here, all I wanted to do was stay at home and watch TV. It helped me learn English—the game shows especially helped me to increase my vocabulary.

Life here is very different in many ways. Relationships here are less formal. I've had to learn to say no because otherwise my husband won't know my feelings, which is the American way. There is not as much courtesy in American marriage. My husband goes to sleep without even saying good night. It's very casual here—sometimes it seems rude to me. It gives me an empty feeling. I don't have confidence to have a child yet, because everything seems so new. I like to watch Phil Donahue and Oprah Winfrey because people talk about the same problems in their marriages that I have in mine, and it makes me feel less isolated and alone. Even if I take a walk on the sidewalk, there is no one to say "good day" to. Everyone is either jogging or riding in their car.

When I read a book, I feel so empty because even though I can read the words, I can't always grasp the content because English is still so new to me. I'm trying to live my life in English, but it's frustrating because I know I'm missing so much. It's like my brain works much faster than my language. I always carry a dictionary with me so when I have an idea or feeling, I can look up the word. I look forward to the time when I can express myself freely. Already I am less shy, just from living here.

Henriette Vrabie

My husband was invited to the University of Virginia in 1984. We both had good professorships at the university in Rumania. We had plenty of material comfort, but we felt constrained and wanted more freedom not only for ourselves but for our youngest daughter. I have a married daughter, who stayed behind in Rumania, which was very hard. Besides leaving our oldest child behind, the hardest thing for us about leaving the country to start over again at our age is we have to learn to do without certain comforts in our lives that we had always been used to. For the first time we have very little because we had to start with nothing but ourselves.

My husband came here three years before us. A friend of his got him a job here, but it was not so simple for my daughter and me to leave the country. It was very difficult time for me. I lost my professorship and was demoted to librarian. I had a lot of pressure from officials to divorce my husband of thirty-three years. During that time I studied my English in preparation for teaching when I arrived in America. I was sure I could get a job teaching French because French was the first language of my childhood. I didn't realize that my résumé wouldn't have much value here because I hold no degrees from an American university. When we finally got here, it was a shock for me to discover that Americans seem to fairly worship youth. It's hard to get a job in academics when you are over forty-five. It's a shame because I feel like I'm a better teacher now than I was at thirty-five. It is very discouraging to be willing to work and not have the chance. In Europe you are respected for your experience, but here they seem to hold your years against you. Frankly, I some-times get depressed, but I can't honestly say I have regrets because my husband's career is definitely better off professionally working here. I don't think I was prepared for the sacrifices we've had to make. I had no idea how much I would miss my relatives. Of course, I've only been here less than a year and I know it takes time. Already my fourteen-year-old daughter seems to be totally adjusted to her new life. She is making good grades in school. In Europe your family name is a very important part of your identity. I hope that in America my daughter will be able to succeed solely on her individual merits because obviously her family name isn't very well known over here.

For me, the hardest part of immigration is loss of the intellectual stimulation of an academic life. I teach private French lessons now, but this is a small town with limited opportunities for tutoring. I don't want any help from anyone but a chance to work. As a new immigrant, you feel very insecure. You are alone in the world. I am afraid that I came too late in my life to start over. It's very frustrating when you can't use the skills you spent a lifetime acquiring.

The best part about living here is you can be more relaxed and live a more natural life. You don't have to think about everything you say. You are free to express your true feelings and not be afraid of repercussions. Here you can be interested in politics and be honest about it. You can be true to yourself and are not forced to be a hypocrite. I hesitate to discuss the stresses of the daily life I left behind because I have my family there that I want to protect. It's probably difficult for Americans to understand how words can be used against you.

Genevive Francisco

My parents immigrated to America when I was four, and I grew up with my grandparents in the Philippines. They found that life in the United States was so hard they wouldn't be able to support their daughters, so we had to stay behind. All my life America was like a dream to me—the place where I always wanted to go. As a child I really thought money grew on trees here. I studied English in the Philippines in preparation for coming here, but when I finally got here after high school, I was too shy to speak for a while. When I got to my father's in San Fancisco, I couldn't get over how many people had microwaves and VCRs. At first it was strange to call my mother "mother" because I could hardly remember her. She seemed more lively, liberated, and free than the mothers in the Philippines. I miss my grandparents and hope that they can visit this year. I don't think my mother has regrets about letting our grandparents raise us because we are much more self-disciplined than American girls. I was amazed how easy it was to get a job as a seventeen-year-old girl. It's easier than it is for a college graduate in the Philippines. My mother became an architect here in America. That would be very difficult for a woman in the Philippines. My sister and I were raised to be shy, and it was hard for me at first to make eye contact and shake hands. Americans are very direct and straightforward. You certainly have much more opportunity if you make eye contact. It was hard to make friends until my mom encouraged me to smile and be friendly. Now, I'm used to it, but my nerves were a mess at first. The skin was peeling off my hands. Things happen faster here because everyone is so direct. Americans tell you how they feel. I enjoy being in college here because you can learn much quicker because of the directness.

It's important to me to establish my own career before I get married or have children, so I can always be financially independent. I'm too proud to be dependent. You can't be an equal if you are dependent, the relationship is out of balance. Even though I want to be independent, I'm very ladylike in my behavior. I don't believe in casual sex, I have more self-respect than that. It's the one American freedom that I think can be very damaging. People here don't seem to have much respect for themselves, the way they give away their bodies and abuse drugs. People here seem to be afraid of commitment.

My ideas about love and marriage have roots in a more traditional culture. I have big goals for my future. After I graduate from the Fashion Institute of Technology I'd like to travel around the world, then settle down in the United States and start my career in interior design. I'm a very ambitious person—I want to be very successful. I don't even let myself think about the possibility of failure.

If I had stayed in the Philippines, I'd have to be a housewife dominated by my husband. When my mother left us, I think I got the idea that I wanted to become famous. I wanted to become someone who would always be remembered. I wanted to have an impact through my creative work, and I really believed that the United States was the best country for big dreams.

The Right Reverend Benoni Y. Ogwal-Abwang

I was born, raised, and educated in Uganda. I was a bishop of the Episcopal Church there. I went to a boarding school where the archbishop presided. He was a tremendous influence on me and influenced my going to the theological college. When Idi Amin came into power in the early 1970s, the archbishop was perceived as his enemy because he was immensely popular. I believe that Idi Amin himself killed the archbishop. He could not stand for anyone to have authority but himself. It was a great shock for me. I had just become bishop and taken over the northern diocese directly from the archbishop. I knew my safety was not secure. I felt the country's main hope was a Christian perspective. Of course, Amin worked to establish Islam in the country. He sent soldiers up north to get me. Literally, as they were breaking down the front door I was running out the back door. I escaped to safety by walking over twenty miles of mountain ranges. I had a priest and a guide with me who helped me get to Kenya. My wife was arrested and questioned but eventually got across the border into Kenya. There was a terrible lot of bitterness in these years. I lost not only my mentor, the archbishop, but my brother was also executed simply because he was my brother. My ministry has taught me a lot about reconciliation and forgiveness. It wasn't easy to let go of hard feelings. I eventually returned to Uganda to try and help the spiritual needs of my war-torn country. There were a lot of widows and orphans to care for, and I met with some success, but in the meanwhile Ugandans had learned new tricks with guns. Within three years of Amin's downfall, there was another military coup. Once again I saw Christians persecuted and beaten. By last year I was again perceived as an enemy of the state, and I knew I had to get out. I've been in the United States for about nine months. My official residence and the theological college in Uganda have been destroyed by this new military government.

The great religious freedom in the United States is its greatest gift to the people. Man is a spiritual being, whether he goes to church or not. He needs some kind of spiritual approach to life. It's a basic part of humanity that can't be denied. My American congregation is predominantly white, whereas in Uganda it was mostly black, but the service is basically the same, even though they are spoken in different languages.

America is the champion of human rights. The people here have really helped me and my family feel good about our lives again. When you go to sleep at night, you know that no one is going to knock on your door and request for your life. Everyone on the streets speaks to me in a friendly fashion. I had heard that the South was not so friendly to blacks, but that has not been my experience at all. People seem so kind and caring here, I've felt nothing but acceptance and support since we've been here. I feel very grateful that there is a place like America that will open its heart to people who have lost their homeland. I don't know how long I will be here, but I accept God's will. After years of rejection, it's wonderful to be accepted.

Zarina Sidi

Growing up in Kenya I never thought about the United States, but after I was divorced, I began to want to travel. I never left Africa until 1983. After several vacations in Europe, I decided to take a home-attendant job in Italy as a nurse. Later, when the opportunity came up to do nursing in America, I was excited for the opportunity. I've only been here four months. I was afraid that blacks would be mistreated, but I think discrimination is less here than in Italy. I really like it here. I've started taking college courses. The people here are much more friendly and accepting than at home. Society seems much less segregated. Wages here are almost twice as much for the same work in Kenya. I've never had much trouble meeting people, and Americans are very open and friendly. It's funny, growing up in Kenya I always thought of skyscrapers and cowboys in America, whereas there are neither in the town where I'm working. I enjoy wearing my traditional Kanga while I'm here, it's like a little piece of home I can take with me.

Being here isn't as difficult as being in Italy, because I speak the language. I think I've always been an ambitious person. I've always set goals for myself and am curious to know more. Right now, my education is very important to me. Besides taking college courses, I'm reading a lot of American history I enjoy home-nursing care, but I'm always thinking of doing other things as well. I'm thinking about starting a children's magazine. I really don't know how long I'll stay in the United States. I try to leave myself open to any possibilities in the future. I'm somewhat of a tomboy. I prefer to compete myself rather than watch others play the game.

Roeun Om

My husband and I were farmers in Cambodia. I was seventeen when we were married. Our parents arranged the marriage. I knew him all my life because we were from the same village. I thought then I'd be a farmer's wife for my whole life. I was content to live the same life that my mother and grandmother had lived. I never thought I'd leave my village, much less the country, to come to the United States. When war broke out in my country, my husband was a soldier, and I would follow him as much as I could. We were forced to leave our village by the Khmer Rouge. I knew we would die if we tried to stay on our farm. We lost a lot of my family in the war. My second child died in the refugee camp. I was glad to travel to America because I thought the farther we got away from the war, the safer my family would be. I am afraid to die. I had never been on an airplane before. I got sick to my stomach. I lost my shoes and didn't know one word of English, but we just smile and say yes. I never cooked with electricity or had a refrigerator before I was in the United States. Now I can drive a car. The church that sponsored us to come here met us at the airport. They help us get shoes, get jobs and a house. We've been here three and a half years now, but my English is still not so good. We work hard for money to pay the bills. Life is the same everywhere that way. I still feel fearful sometimes because of the terrible things I saw people do to each other in Cambodia. I try not to think about it, but I still do. When we lived on a farm, before the war, it was easier to feed the family than it is here now. But the war and killing changed all that, and our past is gone. Now I work many hours in a hotel laundry to buy food and pay the rent. My husband works until late at night. It's hard when school starts because my oldest son won't be able to take care of my little one. I can't afford to quit my job and I can't leave my five-year-old alone after school. I don't know what I'll do. Every night I wake up in bed and worry. I don't think I'm brave. My husband carried me out of the country in his arms when I was pregnant with my baby. He is the brave one. He climbed down into the lime pits and pulled out two children that were still alive and saved their lives. I cried and cried when the Communists were shooting at our backs as we ran. My husband yelled at me to keep going.

Now we have another chance at life, but it is not easy to support our family. Rent is very expensive. I hope we can stay in our house, but I'm fearful we will have to move. I know my sons probably won't marry Cambodians. We are Americans now. If I could speak good English, I would feel more like an American. My children learn in school. They like hamburgers and rock and roll. It's hard to learn English when you're doing laundry all day. I don't have much time to watch TV, because when I'm home I have to cook for my family. It's hard to sleep, not because I fear for my life, but I'm afraid we won't have enough money to pay the bills. Little girls work hard in Cambodia helping their mothers with the housework, so I always knew that life is hard work. I'm not afraid of hard work, only of failure to take care of my family. Right now I don't feel ambitious, I just want not to lose what we have. I don't spend much time thinking about being rich, I'm too busy trying to hold on to what we've done so far. I don't know what I'll do if I cannot find someone to watch my little boy after kindergarten. If I lose my job, we can't pay the rent, then where will my family go?

Eskiender "Alex" Mehari

I go by Alex because Eskiender is the first name of Alexander the Great. I grew up in Addis Ababa and came to the United States in 1971 to go to school. I lived with a family in California as an exchange student. It wasn't such a hard transition for me because I went to an American school in Ethiopia, so I spoke English, wore American clothes, and listened to rock and roll growing up. The biggest adjustment in living here is getting used to how fast things move, how quickly people think and talk. Once you get used to the pace, you can become a real American. I got a scholarship to college in Minnesota and graduated in 1976. I wanted to go to law school, but the political situation in Ethiopia got so bad that my parents couldn't afford it, and I had to start making a living. Going home was not an option. My family's business was "nationalized," and my father was put in jail. The pressure of losing everything he'd worked for eventually killed him.

I got into the hotel business over the years. I like the immediate satisfaction of the results and the cash in your pocket. I started as a waiter in Washington, D.C., and eventually got a job in Houston as room service captain. I just got married a couple of days ago. I can't believe how easy it is to get married here. My brother and I bought a house last summer and we just opened an Ethiopian restaurant, so I'm working over seventeen hours a day right now on two jobs This is a very exciting time in my life. Two years from now I'd like to see myself running a successful business. If this restaurant isn't it, something else will be.

Ethiopians in general are shy and humble people. These are not characteristics that will take you very far in America. I've had to force myself to be more aggressive because that is the way things are done here and this is my country now. It is an adjustment to change your culture and it takes time. The color of my skin has probably been an obstacle for me from time to time, but I've never felt like it was an obstacle I couldn't overcome. My children will have an advantage over me in that this will be their culture. They won't have to relearn how the world works.

I think this is the best place in the world to be. You can be yourself here in a way that's impossible in many other countries. There is enough work here for you to do if you're willing to work. If you have plans and goals in your life, you have the best chance of playing them out here. You can even create your own job and your own religion if you want. You don't get bogged down in tradition. Life-styles are much more flexible here. I think in general Americans are optimistic, hardworking, and independent. The pioneer spirit still exists very strongly in this country. I'm an American now. I feel like a modern-day pioneer.

Jung Ae Kweun

I lived in Seoul, Korea, all my life until four years ago when I came to the United States. My mother's sister married an American and invited my family to come and live near her. Now all my family is here. No one is left in Korea. We all want to come here because it is better to make the money in the United States. The harder I work, the more money I make. I work twelve hours a day, sometimes seven days a week. We sell fresh food and flowers. We have nine people from my family working in the green grocery. My family has several stores now. I have a new baby, but I have to keep working. My mother's friend takes care of my boy. In Korea, women have to stay home and take care of husbands and babies, but here it is different—we work to make the money. Life is not only about money, but we need it and that is why we are here. Maybe I make enough money so my son won't have to work so hard. This country gives you a chance to make things better for your children if you work hard. My son can get a good education and do anything he wants. I think it is important for my son to go to college. My English is still not so good, but already I dream in English as well as Korean. Since I was a child, I always heard the American world was very beautiful. We study English in school. When I came to the United States, I was a little shocked how dirty it is, but now I am used to it. Korean people like things very clean. That is one reason our stores do well is because we wash, wash, and try to make everything perfect. We try very hard to make things nice.

No matter how long I live here, some things I think I will never get used to. I do not like to see boyfriend and girlfriend hug and kiss in public. I also do not understand why Americans don't take care of their parents when they are old. There is too much freedom here, not enough rules—no self-control. Koreans do not get divorced, they stay together and take care of their families. I want to raise my son with Korean custom of respect and responsibility.

Adam Hryniewicki

I came here a couple of years ago. I always wanted to come to America. My mother told me that if I want to leave Poland, Germany is for Germans and France is for the French, but the United States is for everyone. From my graduating class of thirty in Danzig, there are only about ten people left in the country. All the ambitious young people have to leave if they want to achieve their goals. It's a shame for my country, but you can't control people and keep them satisfied. I came to America with a round-trip ticket, but I knew I would want to stay here. There was no way I could stay in Poland. The only way to have a nice life there is to be a bad person—totally corrupt. Here in America I can make a nice life for myself and mind my own business.

Even though I knew no English, I found a Polish man who gave me a job after I'd been here for about six weeks. I worked sometimes ten to twelve hours a day for not much pay. All I did was work and sleep. Later I met another man who would pay me by the hour, which seemed a lot more fair. Being an electrician, it's pretty easy for me to find work. I'm lucky to have a skill that translates into English. It's very hard to get a license in New Jersey, but I work as a subcontractor for a licensed electrician. I get paid pretty well. I'm beginning to do painting and carpeting and carpentry as well.

I feel a lot less frustrated living here. I feel like I have more control over my future. Good ideas are valued here. A lot of people get rich off a clever idea. The key to success here is to maintain your focus. You lose your focus and you lose yourself. Anything you want is here, if you know what you want. The little things like the food you eat and the clothes you wear—there are so many choices. One thing I really like about this country is knowing people from different backgrounds. I don't want to live only in a Polish community. I want to assimilate, but I was born and educated in Poland and will always be a Polish-American. I can make a lot of money here in a very short time, but the quality of life in the Northeast is not so nice. After I've saved up some money, I'd like to travel to other parts of the country and maybe settle in the South or the West.

One American habit I don't understand is buying on credit. I don't believe in working so hard just to pay off the interest and you still have your debt. America is a factory of interest. I never buy anything unless I can pay for it. I don't want to owe anyone anything because then I wouldn't be a free man. It's unbelievable to me that American parents charge their grown children rent to live at home. I don't understand this attitude toward money. If you care about money too much, it's hard to be a kind person.

Maria Haritou

I was teaching in Greece when I saw an application for working abroad. I was at a point in my life where I was looking for something new. I was ready to try other things. I wanted so much to break out of a mold, do something different. I did not want to think and act like a civil servant for my whole life. America was a chance for me. I always wanted to come to New York. It is the metropolis of the world. It is like a big clock that strikes time for the whole world. Of course, I was homesick at first. After all, it was the first time in my life I was alone. In a way, I needed to get away from my parents because even though I love them very much, they were an obstacle for me. They were afraid for me to come here, but they know New York also holds many opportunities for me. After two years I feel like I know the city better than most New Yorkers. My English gets better all the time even though I speak Greek most of the day during my job at the consulate. I feel a bit divided, a bit apart. I feel a split between traditional and contemporary life. Part of me belongs here, but part of me is rooted in Greece for inspiration. I have thought so much, so deeply about myself and what I want to do since I have lived here. Being so alone has given me room to think. My loneliness does not lead me to despair, but to creative action and thinking I can accept everything bad and good at the same time. That is why the United States suits me. The city, especially, has a harmony of antithesis. New York is different from all the other capitals of the world. I would like so much to travel over all of the United States. A European has an ability to experience America in a totally different way than someone who was born here. My Greek culture is very old with a vast continuous history that has been passed down from generation to generation. It appeals to me to be in a new country with new ideas. I do not want to lose my cultural inheritance, but I want to assimilate it and push it forward. I cannot just be an admirer of the past. I must live in the present and plan for the future. I can never just accept. I am for energy and change.

Gunilla Thorberg Godfrey

I got really restless in an office job as a secretary in Sweden, and I thought it might be interesting to travel as a flight attendant. I was very excited the first time I had a flight to America. I was amazed how big everything was—big cars, big buildings, and big hamburgers. Even the policemen in Chicago were big and muscular. My next trip to the United States was to Los Angeles and to Disneyland and Marine World. I really enjoyed my life-style, traveling all over the world. I remember when I was a little girl my paper doll was a stewardess. I was very independent as a child, and my parents' friends used to say that I would do something different from the other children when I grew up. I met my American husband on one of my flights. Living in Texas is much different from Sweden. I miss the forests and mountains and all the water that I grew up with, but I like the American people very much. They are so warm and friendly, it is hard to stay a stranger for long. I miss my parents and sisters, but I love the opportunity I have here in the United States to meet so many different kinds of people. I have had to make an effort to make friends, and probably that has been good for me. Even though women here are more sociable and outgoing than in Sweden, I feel like they are also more private—maybe because of their religious background. It is hard to replace the closeness of the friends you had before you are married and have children. It seems like a wife is much more important here in the United States than she is in Sweden. Couples in Sweden seem more independent. Separate vacations are much more unusual here than in Sweden. Americans seem to really cherish the concept of couplehood.

I think I would like to work again, but I'm not sure what I'd like to do yet. The children are still so small, it will be a while. It seems it is more difficult to be a mother of young children here in America than it is in Sweden. Here women have fewer options. They must lose their jobs or leave their children as soon as they are born. There is much better maternity leave and day care back in my country. In this way, the United States is less modern, I think. I think I surprised myself not only by leaving my work, but by leaving my childhood family and country for my marriage and my children. I have a very different life-style now. I am still not used to being financially dependent. Somehow, though, I have always managed to do what I have wanted to do, so in that way my life hasn't changed.

When I go back to Sweden to visit now, I realize how positive and friendly Americans are. In comparison, Swedes seem rather stiff. I think living here has made me more optimistic and relaxed. I was raised to listen and not ask questions, while American children are encouraged to be open and curious. I like the open and curious attitudes here. I used to sometimes watch "Dallas" on TV in Sweden before I moved to Texas. Now I find myself often at big, big parties with tents and servants. The scale of everything is so grand, just like on TV.

Eng Mu Peung

All my life I lived in Cambodia until the Communists took over the country and starved my family. I don't even know where my husband is buried. I lost two children and eight brothers and sisters. I was forced to work in the rice fields for the Communists. When I finally escaped the labor camp and made it back to the city five years later, our house was destroyed and we had no money. I found a few pieces of zinc and made a little shelter for me and my brother and child. I really didn't want to leave my country, and I tried so hard to stay, but finally I couldn't take it anymore. I carried my eight-year-old child three days and three nights through the jungle to get to the border of Thailand to find the Red Cross to get food and blankets. The forest was filled with land mines and bandits. The border was just as dangerous because the Thais didn't want the refugees and they killed a lot of people. I stayed in a refugee camp there for safety. After seven or eight months I saw my name on the emigration list. I couldn't believe it. I was so excited to finally have a chance at life. I always heard that America was a rich country, so that was my first choice. I studied English for three months in a refugee camp in the Philippines while waiting for a sponsor. My son had never been to school until we came to the United States because my country had been torn apart since he was a baby. It was hard for him at first, but he likes it here very much. We've been here almost seven years. At first I was so sad and lonely without any relatives, and I didn't have any money and couldn't speak English. A while later my sister and brother came over here too and my English got better.

I've had my cleaning job at the hotel for five years now. This country has been good to me. My son is getting a good education. I have a car, plenty to eat, and a place to live. I have two jobs because I am a widow with a child and need the money. My son is a teenager now and I don't have to look after him so much, so I work nights at the hotel and mornings at a private house. I'd like to go to school myself but there is no time. I took my citizenship test last year and should get my papers soon. That will be a big day for me.

My son is a good boy. He helps me with my cleaning job on the weekend. Sometimes I really miss my husband and children, and I can go to the Buddhist temple here in town and it helps me a lot. I never knew I would be working two jobs. The Cambodian custom is for the woman to stay home after she is married, especially after she has a child. I don't have to worry about my son, though, because he doesn't want to cause trouble. We've been through a lot together and have a safe life now. Neither one of us wants to do anything to risk what we've built up for ourselves.

Duma Ndlovu

I grew up in one of the poorest townships in Soweto. When I was a boy, the government took away my father's house and land, and we were forced to move to Phiri. As a child I never questioned why the whites were rich and the blacks were poor. I just accepted things as the way they were supposed to be. I didn't realize that white children had cleaner faces and clothes because our own mothers spent virtually all their time keeping them that way. I thought it was the will of God. My mother made fifty dollars a month as a domestic servant, and I have had to work ever since I was a young boy. When I was in high school and was exposed to world history and reading in English, reality began to change for me. I began to question. I started calling whites "Sir" instead of "Master." By the late 1960s the idea of black consciousness was spreading around the world. Martin Luther King, Jr., was killed, and Muhammad Ali was jailed for draft evasion. Steven Biko had just emerged as a vibrant voice for South African blacks. Students began to protest apartheid. The real evil of apartheid is that it has taught people that blacks are inferior beings. The system is inferior, not the people.

Once our consciousness was raised to this truth, we realized that we could overcome our oppression. By my early twenties I was part of a poetry group that read at political rallies, and I worked as a journalist. After Steven Biko was killed, I read poetry at his funeral, then went to do readings at three other universities. When I returned to South Africa, the police were looking for me. I couldn't go home or to relatives and had to hide out. All my friends were raided. My brother was arrested simply because he was my brother. My poetry group and newspaper were banned. It was becoming more and more impossible for me to function within South Africa. Although I hated the idea of living in exile, I felt like I could do a lot more good living as a free man in America than jailed in South Africa. I got a scholarship to Hampton Institute, in a small town in Virginia that was so provincial that the restaurants closed for lunch. While still in South Africa I had read the writings of Stokely Carmichael, Malcolm X, and Angela Davis, so I was aware that America was far from perfect, but it still offered me an opportunity to educate the world to the atrocities of racism. Most people in Virginia, black or white, didn't even know what was going on in South Africa, but New York City was like a breath of fresh air. I met black people who not only knew about apartheid but identified with Africa. The police were always pulling me over because I looked "suspicious." We were turned away from clubs and discos. I saw an interracial couple jeered at; so, although I was free, I was not exactly free. The racism here is more difficult to identify and fight against. At least in South Africa we were in the majority, and the enemy is clearly identified in the institution of apartheid. Here you fight shadows.

The way to make the world a better place is to do what we do best. I use culture as an effective weapon. By producing South African theater, poetry, music, and dance for American audiences, I can raise the consciousness of the world more effectively than with a raised fist and political rhetoric. I consider myself a cultural ambassador for my people. The South African theater festival at Lincoln Center was very well received and gave people a lot more empathy for my cause of human rights. That is my goal in this country—to spread the word about the right of human dignity and respect for all people. I live here in exile, but South Africa is my home. I'm a cultural nationalist. I think it is very important for all people to have racial pride, but not at the cost of hating others who are different. No group should build themselves up at the expense of others. I don't want my children to straighten their hair or lighten their skin. We should love ourselves for who we are.

Miguel Torres

It's not hard to spend all your money here because there is so much to buy. In the Dominican Republic there are not so many ways to spend your money. I've tried to raise myself up and save for my future, but it is hard. It seems like the more I make, the more I owe. I've got to make a hundred dollars a day just to pay my loan to the bank. I gotta work every day to try and stay out of debt. I have a lot of pressure, a lot of debt. I owe money for my house, money for my cab. I never can relax, even on Sunday. My ex-wife spends all my money on her friends from Santo Domingo. She got me so in debt I have to struggle not to get behind on my payments. Every dollar I make I owe to the bank. I'm up at three-thirty in the morning, seven days a week, driving my cab. I have loans out to pay my loans. My debt is without end.

In this country you can make a lot of money, but if you don't know how to manage your money, that's big trouble. When you're young and ambitious you want to believe you can get rich quick—but you can get yourself in trouble with your dreams. In the restaurant business I lost more than $200,000. I lost my house in Puerto Rico and one of my taxi medallions, so now I've got to try and build myself up again. You get tired working so hard to pay off your debts when you know you're not putting anything away for the future, but working hard helps me not give up. I am a money machine, my meter is running and I'm paying off my debts. I'll never give up and file for bankruptcy. I've got too much pride. So many people in New York have a hard heart, but I can still laugh and get along. I'm not afraid, even at three or four in the morning, I'll be out on the street with my meter running and a positive attitude.

I never would have had the courage to take out a loan for my taxi's medallion if I didn't believe in myself. The greatest power you have is your mind. You've got to believe in youself to be a success. If you're sitting in my cab trying to get to the airport thinking you're going to miss your plane, you probably will get left behind, but if you believe you're gonna make it, you have a much better chance of catching that plane.

Sissy Min

We both came from families of immigrants. Our parents and grandparents emigrated from China to Burma. Although we were born in Burma, we were raised with many Chinese traditions. We were used to being outsiders, different from the majority. We weren't as accepted as citizens in Burma as we are here. We're probably much more likely to lose touch with our Chinese culture here in America because we feel more accepted in the general population. Our daughter was born here, and she will probably marry an American because she's an American.

It's not unusual for the Burmese to want to come to the United States because job options are so much better here. Everyone in Rangoon takes an aptitude test, and your future career is based on the results. I would have had to be a teacher if I didn't emigrate, even though I didn't really want to teach. When you first come here, you have to swallow your pride and take any job you can get to support yourself while you learn English. We were only allowed to take fourteen dollars out of the country when we left. Now I've gotten training in computer software and I really like my job. My main problem has been finding good child care for my daughter while I'm working. I'd love to have my parents, brothers, and sisters come here to live. It's hard to be so far away from your family. That first year in a new country is tough. It's like you've been dropped on the moon—no common language, no friends or relatives. It's hard on a marriage to rely on your husband to be everything to you. We were newlyweds when we came here. The first year was hard, but we're glad we came because now we have good friends, good jobs, and own our own home.

We're really different people from living here seven years. As an immigrant you have to be unusually independent without the resources of friends and family. You learn to make your own decisions and figure things out yourself. When our parents came here to visit, they comment on how much we've changed. Being separated from your parents forces you to grow up in a hurry. I never want to disappoint or worry my parents with my problems when I write home, so I try to think of the positive things in my life. I learned to keep myself busy so I wouldn't feel the loneliness. Over the years, you become a more positive person. Now my life is full.

Ralph Onuogu

I was raised a Christian in Nigeria. That's why I have the English first name. In high school we learned about America, and like most of my friends I wanted to come here and study. I could not get to the United States until almost three years ago, when I was twenty-six, because the Nigerian government makes it difficult for students to study abroad. I couldn't get a good education in Nigeria because the places in the university were reserved for the sons and daughters of the rich. At the same time, if you get good scores on your entrance exams, the government wanted to keep you in Nigeria so they wouldn't lose their brightest young people It was a very frustrating experience, and I felt like the only way I could make a good life for myself was to leave the country. I didn't want to spend my life cleaning the rich man's office, which would have been my only choice in Nigeria if I didn't have an education. I wanted to be sitting in that desk myself.

When I finally got to America, I couldn't believe how expensive the school fees are here. I've had to drop out this semester because of the costs. With my job as a dishwasher, it was impossible for me to pay the out-of-state fees for college, but I've gotten married to an in-state woman and now I think I can pay for classes soon. Two people can live more cheaply than one.

I think it's harder for a black man to be promoted in this country. I work as hard as anyone in the kitchen and never get promoted to a better job. I see white men work at the sinks for a few months, then they are moved to a better job. I've been a dishwasher for a year and eight months now and I still can't get transferred to another department. They tell me I have to stay at the sink because I don't know how to speak English! I've had twelve years of education taught in English, so how do you explain it? I feel if my skin was white I wouldn't be a dishwasher for more than six months. People look at me and think I might be a criminal or a drug addict, and it's unfair because this is not my life-style at all. I am a Christian and I would never put that shame on my family. I work hard like my father before me, and I'm not ashamed of being a dishwasher and working hard for a living. My faith in God gives me the strength to persist in my goals and not get too discouraged. I believe one day I will have a chance to make a good life for myself. I'm not afraid of anything because God is my guide. Even though I've encountered some problems in my life I believe that one day my prayers will be answered.

Angela Farrugia and Mary Sultana

We were born and raised in Malta. Our father was in the merchant navy and he would come back from his travels with clothes and stories from all over the world. This made me and my sister curious about life off the island. We would read the Italian magazines about the American movie stars. My parents came over to the United States to work because we wanted them to, as there were not enough jobs for everybody on Malta, and we thought that in the United States everyone lives like kings and queens. We wanted to live here too, but we had to wait until they had an apartment. They have now retired and have gone back to Malta, but I do not think I will ever go back there to live. My children are American.

Malta is nice but there are no jobs and it is boring. It is a small place, you look out your windows and don't see anyone on the street. It is fifty miles out in the Mediterranean, about the size of Bermuda. You never forget you are on an island.

In America I feel like I have more opportunities to do different things. You can make any kind of life for yourself that you want. We have to work very, very hard here; however, we can save to buy a house and make a nice life for ourselves. Life is hard wherever you go. In this world, you have to work to live, and here in this country there is more work. My work is exciting in a printing plant that makes bonds. I like meeting the people who work here, they come from all over the country, and I enjoy meeting so many different kinds of people. I never feel lonely because there is always someone to talk to.

Maltese families are very close. On that small island you can never get away from one another. Here I like seeing all the people on the street who are strangers because there are very few strangers in Malta. I like the privacy that I have here in this country. I feel like I have more opportunities to choose any life that I want here in the United States. I have more freedom to have my own mind. Even though Manhattan is an island, I miss the water. It is not so easy to get to the beach. It is amazing how time changes you. Sometimes I surprise myself how I can adapt and change and go on. My life is very different here but I am used to it and I do not look back—I always hope for something good, but we never know.

Thang Huynh

After I graduated from navigational college, the war in Vietnam was fighting really hard and I had to join the South Vietnamese army. I worked together with the Americans to keep my country in freedom. Sometimes I'm angry at the United States for leaving us to the Communists in 1973. They were our allies, and they let us down. I was put in a Communist "re-education" camp for over five years. I used to be a bigger man, but all I got to eat for years was a few ears of corn. If my family hadn't gotten food to me from time to time, I definitely would have starved to death. I cannot live without freedom. There is no way the Communists could re-educate me. For many months I dug a tunnel with a spoon so I could escape from the camp. I knew if I could crawl out at night I would have a chance because the Communists couldn't use watchdogs. The prisoners were so hungry, we would eat the dogs. My father paid a fisherman to meet me with his boat even though we knew I'd be killed if I got caught escaping. I would rather die than stay there for the rest of my life. After twenty-six days in the jungle, I made it to a refugee camp in the Philippines. That was years ago, but I still have nightmares today that the Communists are chasing me down.

After about a year in the refugee camp, I was allowed to immigrate to the United States. I arrived in San Francisco in 1982. I was so glad to live in a free country again. All I want is to take care of myself and be free to come and go as I please. In a Communist country, even if you aren't in jail, you feel like you are. You can't go where you want or say what you want. I cannot live in captivity. The American people don't know anything about the Communists. If they did, they would have used more of their B-52 bombers to help save Saigon in 1972. Americans say, "Don't send my husband, don't send my son, don't send my tax dollars." They have no idea what it is like to live without freedom. If they did, they would have done anything to stop the Communists.

I've been here almost six years now. I studied English very hard so I could get a job. First I got a job as a house painter, then I got my job making scenery at the aquarium. I'm able to make enough money to send three hundred dollars a month to my parents in Vietnam. After I work here forty hours a week, I work at a restaurant as a cook nights and on the weekends. I work fourteen hours a day, seven days a week, to feed my parents as well as myself. If I didn't send the money every month, they would starve to death. I don't have any time to have a girlfriend. My parents want me to get married and have a family, but I can't let them starve in their old age.

Asians don't have any trouble getting work. They are willing to take any job and work hard. You can move up very quickly in this country if you work hard. We also know to treat people with respect. It seems like many Americans don't have good manners. They sometimes don't seem to have respect for their parents or their bosses. The Vietnamese are different. We work hard and show respect. Our strong families help us be good citizens.

Varuni Nelson

I was born in Sri Lanka, but as a young child my parents moved to England to complete their medical training. When we moved back to Sri Lanka I had forgotten my Sinhala and could only speak English. I kept up my studies in English even though the government was encouraging classes to be taught in the native language. My family moved to Zambia, in Africa, and there was a lot of resentment against Indians and English-speaking people because the country had recently gained independence. It was not a very pleasant experience. The United States began to look like the best place for us to live because we spoke English and they were looking for doctors. It's almost like I was an immigrant all my life, so I was grateful and happy to go to the United States. I knew the country was more welcoming toward immigrants. After the move, it took me several years to realize that I was living in a country that I wasn't passing through, that I'd stay and become a citizen. I consider myself an American, but I'll wear a sari when I get married next year. I could not see myself in the typical American white wedding veil, even though I wear dresses to work. I know I've really become an American because I'm not nearly as critical of this country's arrogance as I was when I first came here. I used to think it was ludicrous that the World Series was called the World Series when it was only played with American teams. Now I'm such a baseball fan, I don't stop to think about such things.

One way my life will be different here in America for me than it was for my mother is that it was a lot easier for educated middle-class women to work outside the home in Sri Lanka because domestic help was so easily available. Even mothers with young children didn't feel guilty about leaving their babies with someone else while they went out because everyone else did it too. American women seem a lot more confused about being a mother and having a career. It didn't seem unusual at all for me growing up that my mother was a doctor because my parents had met each other in medical school and most of their friends were doctors. Almost all of my childhood friends had live-in domestic help. That seems to be something only the very wealthy have here, and it makes it harder for middle-class women to work outside the home.

I realized by my teens that I was too squeamish to be a doctor, but I'd always loved words and language. I knew it wasn't practical to be a writer, so law school seemed like a good step after college. I'm a lawyer now and I like the intellectual challenge and the security of the work. America is a wonderful country for capable, ambitious people, but a lot of people also fall through the cracks. The upside of this country is it offers different kinds of people different opportunities, but the downside is its complacency about being the greatest country on earth. There's still plenty of room for improvement.

Dagnachew Mengesha

I lived in Ethiopia all my life until I had to get political asylum in Sudan in 1981. I stayed in a refugee camp there until I got a chance to come to the United States in 1984. The government in my country was a big contradiction. It was impossible to live there anymore. All the young, educated people are put in jail.

I could already speak English because I learned it in school. The YMCA in Texas was my sponsor to America. They helped me get a job. It was very hard for me and my wife when we got here three years ago because everything is new. We have a son now and are working hard to save our money, but everything is so expensive that it's not easy. We don't think about our life in Ethiopia because we know that we'll never go back. That life is over, and we're working to build our future.

To be a survivor, you have to think about tomorrow and have no complaints. You can have a good life here. Like everybody else in America, we have modern appliances like television. Only the rich have these things in Ethiopia. Even if you're not rich, Americans have a car and go to a restaurant. Even people without a job have a radio and a toaster. Only wealthy people have these things in Ethiopia. My employer here gives me medical insurance so I went to the doctor for the first time once I lived here. Only the rich went to medical doctors in my country. I guess the American middle class are workers who can have things like the company owners. We will probably never be rich, but I feel like I'll always be able to find a job and take care of my family. This is the most important thing for a man.

Thuhuong Nguyen

I was just a little child during the Vietnam War. I remember the sounds of the bombs—running, running, dead bodies and blood and I don't know where I'm running to. This is one of the earliest memories of my childhood. When I was fourteen years old, my mother told me to go with these people and get on a boat. I didn't know who they were or where I was going, but I was brought up to do what I was told. When I got on the boat, it was horrible—dark and cramped, with no food and water. For six days it was too crowded to even lie down. We finally made it to a refugee camp in Galang. They gave us just enough food to keep us alive. I spent ten months there and it kept getting more and more crowded with refugees arriving every day. All I could do was hold on to the idea of America as a place that would save my life.

I never would have had to leave my home if the Communists didn't take over my country, but I've been here six years now and I don't know if I could be happy in Vietnam again because I'm used to my freedom and running my own life now. I was so happy to be reunited with my brother in Oregon, after being separated from my family for a year. But, I had gotten used to taking care of myself and I didn't want my brother to have to support me, so after I learned better English, I got a job and my high school diploma. I want to go to college but I can't get financial aid because the paperwork is impossible. I've been working long hours every day to save up my money to go to

school. I work so hard, over seventy-five hours a week at the fish store, but at least I get to keep my money instead of giving it all to the Communists. I have so much family still in Vietnam who are in a desperate situation. I send them as much money as I can. It makes it hard to save for college, but I am so much better off than they are that I can't say no to their needs. If I could get a college degree, I could make more money to send them, but it's impossible to save up enough for the tuition. I work six days a week, over twelve hours a day. Sometimes I feel so bad. I'm afraid my life will pass by and I'll never be able to get an education or have a family. My brother in Oregon wants to give me some money for college, but he needs that money for his own family and I really do want to take care of myself I can make more money in California than in Oregon, so for the time being I live apart from my brother. I never want to feel helpless again like I did on that boat when I escaped Vietnam. I was too shy to get any food or water. I was so scared. I don't want to depend on people for anything. I know when I get out of bed in the morning, I can take care of myself.

I like my independence but sometimes it feels a bit lonely. People here aren't so friendly toward me. Sometimes I feel invisible, like they see right through me. Now that I can speak English, I still don't feel totally accepted here. I used to think that it was just a language problem, but I'm afraid the problem is bigger than that. I think some people resent me because I'm Vietnamese.

Peter Rosenberg

When you immigrate, you face your life with a deeper hunger, a stronger desire to improve your life because you've lost the traditional support systems of your family, friends, and culture. When I left Rhodesia at seventeen to come to school in America, I was envied by many of the people I left behind. I always knew I was going to come here. The United States is always the trendsetter and I wanted to be part of the trend. I wanted to live in a country that was economically and politically stable.

At culinary school I enjoyed the kitchens more than management. I started out sweeping the storeroom and worked my way up over the years to the position of head chef. American efficiency and proficiency were real eye-openers to me. In South Africa a tomato is a tomato; here I have a dozen varieties to choose from. I love that—it makes it much easier to be creative. It's very exciting being a chef here. My kitchen is like the U.N. The staff is from all over the world.

One of the biggest adjustments for me was getting used to the working hours here in America. Everyone in Rhodesia quit working at five o'clock and had two months' vacation. Here I work until the job is done and I'm lucky if I can get a week or two vacation. I never seem to have any spare time. I rarely leave the kitchen before eleven o'clock at night. I love my work because you get a lot of instant satisfaction. You see your success or failure right away, and no two days are the same. Executive chefs are a lot younger, now that American regional foods are replacing the heavier European classical cuisine. If you're willing to work hard, you can rise professionally very fast in this country. American cooking is trendsetting and chefs are more experimental in America. It's almost expected of you to create your own individual dishes. I like to be free from the restraints of tradition.

You can't really appreciate what you have until you don't have it. Immigrants lose everything that is familiar in their lives and start all over again. When you've re-established a new life for yourself here, you really treasure it. Things have greater value. I consider myself very privileged to live here. I'm convinced my life is much more fulfilling than if I had stayed in Africa, but I've got two small children and it's hard to work as late at night as I do.

I feel like the opportunity in this country goes as far as I can reach. America wants winners and they give you the encouragement to succeed. I really like the "go for it" attitude here. American children grow up thinking they can be an astronaut or president of the United States if they want to. It's a great attitude.

Julia Del Arroyo

I lived all my life in Lima, Peru, until we came to the United States four years ago. I was a teacher of home economics to high school students there, but it's very hard for my husband and me to find work. After you graduate from university, there are not very many jobs. My oldest daughter was born with a kidney infection and the doctors could not help her. We take her to the United States for medical treatment and the American doctors make her well. We liked it so much here, we want to stay. It's very hard to immigrate here. The government makes it difficult because everyone wants to be American. There are jobs for anyone willing to work. That is the greatest thing about this country. I work as a housekeeper here and have a family to sponsor me for a green card.

It's worth starting over here because in Peru even if you have money, there's often no meat or milk and sugar in the store. It's hard to feed your children well because there is not very much to buy. Right now it is hard for us here because I can't be a teacher until I get my green card, but I know I will and then I'll be able to find work as a teacher. You can make good money in the public schools. I am studying English after my work as a housekeeper. It's not so bad to work as a servant here because the people treat me so well, much nicer than in Peru. They don't look down on me, but say, "sit down and have a cup of coffee." They give me champagne for Christmas and make me feel comfortable.

We moved here for our children. This is the most important thing to South American families. It's strange to me how American families live so far apart. I'm used to everyone being close by. Here everyone is so busy and lives so far away. Women here work hard like a man, and there's no one home to run the family. There's not even a grandmother nearby to watch the children if the mother has to work. I'm not comfortable leaving my girls with a baby-sitter. I take them with me or leave them with my husband. We don't need to be millionaires with a mansion. We want our daughters to have the opportunity to be anything they want to be. This is the most important thing to us. The hardest thing about immigrating is leaving the rest of our family behind. I haven't seen my own mother for over four years.

The biggest change in our lives is how hard everyone works. In South America, people work only until three or so in the afternoon. Here people work until long after dark. You come home and you're tired. It's hardest for the women, because they work hard all day, out of the house like the father, and they have no family nearby to help care for the children, the cooking, and housework. I get more tired here than I ever did in Peru, but it's worth it because I know my daughters will get a good education and a chance of good professional jobs when they are out of school. We might scrub floors now but I believe one day we'll be teaching again and our children will have good opportunity for a happy life. We don't mind the sacrifice we make with our own jobs because we feel if our girls get their American citizenship, that is the best investment we can make in the future.

Bill Dembski

I was born in 1956 in Poland. I graduated from the university in 1978 with a master's in electrical engineering. I had always read about America as the land of opportunity. I guess I'm an ambitious person, but I don't need to be the richest man around. I'm more of a family man than a career man, but I do like adventure and knowing that I'm trying my best, so we decided to try life in the United States. I'll never forget July 14, 1981, when my wife and I landed in New York airport and we looked at each other and said, "What now?" You have your suitcases in your hands and you have to make it somehow. We didn't know anyone here, but we had each other and our whole future ahead of us. Our English was not as good as we thought. My parents had friends in Texas, so we took a forty-five-hour bus ride to Houston. I got a job as a welder right away. One reason immigrants always find a job is they're willing to do any kind of work. You won't find too many unemployed American electrical engineers taking a welding job in the Texas summer heat. They'll just collect unemployment before they'd work with a torch in over 100 degree [heat]. My wife is a master's economist and she took a job at McDonald's for $3.25 an hour. Immigrants have to take what they can get. They have no safety net or an unemployment check. After six months we had a nice apartment and a car. Although our life-style wasn't as nice as what we left behind, I could see the progress we'd made [from nothing] in such a short time that I believed we could make a better future for ourselves here in America than we could back in Poland. Living here gives you a feeling of freedom that you won't find even in Western Europe. I could pick up the phone today and get a job in L.A. if I wanted to. You always have the possibility of rearranging and changing your life. I think that's the main difference for me living here. The downside of that freedom, of course, is that you can get fired immediately if you cross the wrong person. I don't buy on credit because I wouldn't be comfortable being in debt, especially when there is no job security. Every time I give one of my employees a raise, they buy something and get more in debt. I don't understand this. I like to feel free. It's hard to save in this country because it's so easy to buy on credit. A hundred dollars down will buy you a thousand-dollar stereo or whatever. I won't do that because I want to stay a free man.

Now I am head engineer of a hotel, and my wife is manager of a McDonald's. We feel like we have been rewarded for our hard work. We have a daughter now and enjoy taking her to the zoo or playing around the pool on the weekends. Most people in Houston turn on their air conditioners and watch TV. That seems strange to me. You can become a little bit lazy and spoiled by all the American conveniences. People are fatter here because they are always sitting in their car, at work, or at home, snacking in front of their TV. You don't even have to get out of your car to get a meal. Americans don't get enough exercise and there is plenty to eat. All the food is fried and full of sugar and salt. You have to make a real effort to get enough exercise and eat healthy foods here because the average life-style doesn't promote it.

Yolanda Pareja

I lived in Ecuador all my life until I came to this country about seventeen years ago. I never wanted to come here. I don't like this country because the language is very hard for me. I was almost forty-five when we moved here. Some husbands fall in love with another woman, but my husband fell in love with another country. He came here for a visit and liked it so much, he wanted to stay. He says it's so clean, so organized, and he likes the people. He gets a job and wants me to bring the children to live with him in Washington, D.C. My children miss their father, so we came, but I miss my family and my life in Ecuador very much, and I go back to South America after one year. Here everyone is in such a hurry, no one has time to sit and drink coffee and talk about their family. I was so lonely in this big tall apartment, I never see any people except on the elevator and then no one ever speaks to you. When I go back to Ecuador I realize I can't stay because my house and all my belongings are sold. It was a terrible feeling to realize I couldn't go back home—there was no home to go to anymore. All my pictures, books, everything sold. So I came back to the United States and study English, but it is not easy to learn a new language at my age. My children are young and in the public school. They learn quickly.

I always stayed at home in Ecuador, but here you need two incomes to pay the bills. I used to have three maids in Ecuador to cook the food, clean the house, and help with the children. Here I have to do all that myself plus work in the laundry at the Holiday Inn and take care of other people's children on the weekends. My husband is proud and would not like me cleaning for other people, but we needed the money so I didn't let him know about that job. It's not so easy to send children to college here. It takes a lot of money. My youngest child is now in his last year of the university. He will be an architect. It cost $50,000 for his education. We have to live with my daughter now. My husband is retired and we can't pay the rent. The lady I was working for decided to stay home with her children, so I lose my job. It's hard for a woman my age to work from eight in the morning until six in the evening. That's what you have to do to take care of the babies in this country. They also expect you to cook, do cleaning, do everything. It is too much. In Ecuador we have many different people to do these jobs. I'm getting too old to work like that now. Even though I've worked here for seventeen years, I have no medical or retirement pay. I have no social security, no way to live in my old age. My husband is the same. My children all have good jobs, though. That was a dream of mine, that my children will have degrees and professions. In that way I have achieved my dream, but I never dreamed that I would find myself unable to pay my own rent. My husband is still in love with this country today even though we don't know how we're going to live in our old age.

This country is about the money. It's not for me. If you like to push yourself and make the dollars, then this country is fine, but I care more about the quality of life than the quantity of money. I've had to spend every penny I made here. I have nothing to show for all my years of hard work but my children's education. Certainly, I hope their lives will not be so hard for them.

Zhanna Drantyev

Growing up in Russia I was very sheltered about life in the rest of the world. I always felt like my questions were never answered. When I met the man who later became my husband, it was like a window to how life should be. He told me about life in America. Within a matter of months we decided to get married and emigrate. Because he was Jewish, his mother had already immigrated to Israel. She sent him papers to help him get permission to leave the country. My own mother is a simple person, she is happy with whatever she has. She knew I was never satisfied. I was always demanding and curious as a child, and she knew my disposition wasn't suited to communism. I felt like I was living a lie. You have to take the work they give you and not ask questions. I couldn't accept that and she knew it, so my own family wasn't that surprised when I decided to emigrate. I wasn't persecuted or threatened, but I knew I wanted to have more opportunities in my life than Russia had to offer me. The only way to improve your life there is do something illegal and I didn't want that. I felt closed in an impossible circle. Now I feel less repressed, more relieved and in touch with my true nature. Jewish refugee organizations helped us get to America. It was the only place we wanted to go when we left Russia. When we first arrived in New York, it was very depressing. We were totally alone without any friends or relatives. We didn't speak the language and we were very fearful of crime.

When I left Russia, for the first time I realized how isolated we were in the USSR. The fashion and style magazines here were so incredibly creative. I like to see the people on the street with their spiked hair and strange clothes. I love the freedom people have to express themselves. Although freedom also means more crime and offensive behavior, I've lived with censorship and the price is too high. The feeling of freedom that you feel on the streets here is a very special and valuable treasure.

The Jewish relief helped us study English. They wanted to get me a job in a factory, but I didn't come here to do that. I went to vocational school and got a job as a mail clerk on Wall Street even though my English was still very weak. After nine months, I got a better paying job at a bank. I marvel at the freedom to switch jobs here. I stayed at home for a year after I had my child, then I got an even better job at a private school as an administrative assistant. I learned a lot working there for two years. I started to take continuing education classes in design, and I really liked it and did well, so I am now enrolled full time. I'd like to be an interior decorator when I graduate this year.

It's much more difficult here to get good child care. This is a weak point in America. It's difficult for mothers to keep their jobs when they have children. I don't understand why women are punished for having children. I think this country could be more on the side of women and children. Russian day care is much better. They have good playgrounds, medical care, and hot meals and good professional day-care workers. Here the government doesn't acknowledge that children exist or that women need to earn money. In Russia there's less guilt for the working mother because the community takes more responsibility for the children. In America, women are on their own to figure out how to keep their jobs and care for their babies at the same time.

Benjamin Humphrey

I was born in Cambodia, but was sent to Paris as a young boy to be educated. Most people who could afford it sent their children to France for their schooling at that time. I returned to Cambodia for university and military service. I was in the Cambodian diplomatic corps. I was sent to Vietnam to represent the Cambodian and the United States Military. My military career had been closely aligned with America since the 1950s. In 1972 I was transferred to Thailand. On April 17, Phnom Penh was invaded by the Communists and we lost our country. I kept warning my friends and family that Cambodia was going to fall, but no one wanted to believe me. I sent my son to the United States and my daughter to France for their own protection. My wife was with me in Thailand when Cambodia fell to the Communists. I knew we could not go back home again. My entire life was cut off. My mother, my brothers, and neighbors were all left behind and there was nothing I could do about it. The Khmer Rouge would have killed me immediately. I felt like my whole country was murdered, and I was cut in half. Our country was a pawn in a global chess game and we were lost when the United States pulled out of Vietnam. That is a terrible feeling, but fortunately I had good American friends who arranged to send us to the United States. My wife had always been a housewife, but she got a job right away when we relocated to Virginia. We didn't want to be on welfare. We felt that we represented our country and we wanted to have pride. After work we would help other Cambodian, Vietnamese, and Laotian immigrants get settled in the United States. It's very hard because of the language barrier, but they are willing to work hard to improve their lives. After a while I noticed that a lot of the Americans are jealous when they see the recent immigrants in a new car or with a color TV. What they don't realize is that a family gets by on nothing but a bowl of rice and two fingers of fish to save for those things, which represent a new way of life in America. After one year here I had saved enough money for a down payment on a house. We work so hard because we lost everything and have to build new lives for ourselves. A lot of employers like to hire Cambodians because they work so hard. This causes some resentment, but refugees can't help working seven days a week because they are desperate to start their life over again. Work is food, work is life.

Here you can live any kind of life you can make for youself. I decided to change my name when I came here. My last name is Hum, which means "free," so I call myself Humphrey, like Hubert Humphrey or Humphrey Bogart—free like an American. Benjamin is the name of my sponsor, so I took it as a symbolic gesture to be a United States citizen. I think of this country as a host and I feel grateful to be here.

The best thing that Cambodians learn from Americans is how to treat their children. Here you talk to your children and explain things. That is a much better way. Everybody shares ideas here much more freely, not only among their children, but with friends and neighbors too. I like the way people are free to choose the way they want to live. Americans are free to make decisions for themselves because their lives aren't dictated by their parents. Children are raised to make their own decisions. This is a freedom you take for granted if you are born here.

Jill Schutt

My family is third-generation Australian, originally from England. My father was in the army and we were posted here while I was in the fourth, fifth, and sixth grades. When we returned to Australia they called me the Yank. My oldest sister married an American and invited me to come visit her. I stayed so long I ran out of money, got a job and an apartment; then I got a dog and ended up marrying the veterinarian. Now here I am ten years later with my second little American baby on the way. It was remarkably easy for me to immigrate because I was so young; I was just twenty-one, and just starting my life, so all I was leaving behind was my childhood. Both of us grew up in army families, so my husband also has a somewhat outside perspective of this country. He sees what it is and what it's not. I think a lot of American people are very unaware of the rest of the world. They tend to not know other languages or even the history of other countries. This isolation makes them incredibly patriotic. Australians don't sing the national anthem before sports events or pledge allegiance to the flag before class. This sort of patriotism is just taken for granted here. It's not uncommon to see a flag flying in someone's yard here. It would be downright peculiar down under. I sort of like it. This country has a sense of unity that I find very appealing. I also really love the free enterprise system of capitalism here. The creeping socialism in Australia is deadening to me. I'm awfully glad I moved here. I think I would have been in a much more uninspired rut if I hadn't immigrated. My friends back home live pretty much the same life as their parents do. The men there are much more chauvinistic. My brothers are very much like my father in their attitudes about women. I find myself doing things that I never would have dreamed of doing if I had stayed in Australia. I ran the business end of my husband's veterinary practice, doing things I had no idea I could do. I've never been so torn in my life as I have been since I've been staying at home with my baby. I miss working outside the home, but I know it's only a couple of years. This society really encourages and supports the entrepreneur, but the mother of young children is left pretty much on her own. There is such a large diverse population here that the possibilities for businesses are endless. If you can dream it up and are willing to work hard, you can probably make it happen. It's corny but true that America is the land of opportunity. That's the American way. I suppose I really like the self-confident aggressiveness of so many Americans. I'm spoiled by American conveniences. You can cash a check or make a phone call in a snap. The downside of the efficiency is American's tendency to stereotype. It's as if they need to put each type of person in a certain category.

Yacov Wrocherinsky

I come from a long line of wanderers. Both my parents and grandparents emigrated. When I was born in Argentina, I was given a Hebrew name and a Spanish name. My family moved to Israel when I was twelve. Some of my friends call me Eddie since I moved to America three years ago.

The interesting thing is all my sisters and brother married Americans who were living in Israel. After I got my degree in business, I really wanted to come to the States to see my girlfriend, who had moved there. I loved it the first time I came to visit five years ago. Although I broke up with my girlfriend, I knew I wanted to come back to America to work. I looked at this country as a personal challenge. I felt like my opportunities for success were limited in Israel, while the United States attracted me like a magnet. I was like an athlete in training preparing to come to the United States. For a year I studied computers and practiced English. The first two months here were really hard. My English was not as good as I hoped, and I didn't have a place to live. The first time I went to Macy's, it was so big I couldn't handle it. I went to a corner and fell asleep. Luckily I had joined a program in Israel that helps place international students in jobs abroad. I got a job working for IBM. When I look back on that first year, I don't know how I did it. Just wearing a suit every day took some getting used to. I spent between five and six hours a day commuting on the train. All I did was commute and work. It was my first experience with a large corporation. The people were nice but I felt like I had to perform better than anyone else. I felt like I had to be better than average because I was a foreigner. My second year here I got a fascinating job working computer graphics for the drug scientists at Hoffman-LaRoche. They sent me to management seminars every couple of weekends. It was a fantastic learning opportunity, but always in the back of my mind I wanted to work for myself. I'm much more suited to be an entrepreneur than an employee. It's not just that I wanted to keep the profit; I wanted to have control over my daily life. Six months ago a friend from IBM and I started our own computer consulting firm. I really enjoy the creativity of designing individual computer systems for companies and institutions and teaching people how to use them. Sharing information is part of my philosophy of life. I teach people how to get access to information. Access to information is contemporary knowledge.

The crazy thing is, when I quit my job at the drug company, I was not scared. I know my business will be a success. I really believe there is enough for everybody. There is an abundance of money around. A good idea and hard work will help you tap into it. Already I can feel the momentum of my efforts in the last six months. When I see millionaires in their early thirties, I think to myself, If they can do it, so can I.

My mind is working all the time. I often have to get up in the middle of the night and write things down. My ideas wake me up. I don't know what drives me, but I know I like to take different roads to work each day because I'm always trying to figure out the shortest distance between two points. It's amazing what is possible if you focus on a goal.

Astrid Bailey

Growing up in South America I felt like there was no liberation for the woman. A woman can only do what a man tells her to do. When you get married, you have to obey your husband. If he tells you to stay home with the children, you can't go out and work. I knew early on that I wasn't going to settle for that. When I went to the University of Lima, there were only two women in my class, and we weren't allowed to wear pants. My father was against my education, but my mother would push me to continue my studies. My mother got married young and stayed home taking care of the family, but she always had dreams of being a doctor. When I wanted to go to the university, my father says, "What for?," but my mother encourages me to hold on to my dreams. Once when my father was working out of town, my mother got a job feeding poor children breakfast at school. She loved the work and was very happy, but when my father came back he made her quit and stay home. She gave up her job without a fight. Even though I was a little girl at the time, that had a big impact on me and I knew I would have to escape that kind of oppression. My mother worked very hard all her life and was never paid for the things she did. My father was like most Peruvian men, he took her for granted. My father doesn't even stir the sugar in his coffee. My mother does everything for him.

I met an American and fell in love with him, so I left the country for the first time with him. Later on I went to America with my father. When it was time to go home, I told him I was going to stay. He knew I was in love and there was no arguing with me. I got married, and now I've been here eleven years. I think I could only be happy with an American husband. After I had a child, though, I had some of the same problems my mother had. I thought my husband was totally liberated, but after the baby came, he reminded me of my father. He's telling me, "Astrid, how can you leave your little baby?" He said he'd stay home with our son if I could go out and make as much money as he did. Of course, he knew that was impossible, so I had to stay home until my son started school. This is why I have only one child. I love my son very much, but it was very boring for my mind to be alone every day in the house for years on end. I like being a mother much more now that he is older and going to school. I think motherhood is the hardest job in the world.

Americans take the richness of this country for granted because they've never been without. Only the immigrants can really appreciate the abundance in this country. There is so much comfort here and most people are cynical about our leaders. The United States would be a much better country if the Americans cared more about politics, but everyone is too fat and happy to be aware.

Maura Mulligan

There aren't a lot of jobs or educational opportunities in Ireland, and it's not that uncommon for families to send their children to relatives in America. When I first arrived here at sixteen, everything seemed too big—even the people. It was somewhat overwhelming. My first job here was as a long-distance operator. I was living in Queens with my uncle and commuting to Manhattan. I was instructed not to look at anyone on the street or speak to strangers. After living in a small village where everyone knew me, it was a hard adjustment, but I liked my job with the phone company. My home away from home was the Irish dancing school that I joined. It helped me maintain my identity in the world I left behind. Even after five years, I couldn't adjust to American culture—especially the men. I couldn't stand the way they looked at us, as if we were meat, when I would go to dances. I didn't think I'd ever adjust, so I retreated by joining a convent. I wore a habit for seventeen years. In the convent I got my high school and college degrees and got my teaching certificate. Over the years I came to realize that I couldn't continue my personal growth there—that I had to wake up and rejoin the [secular] world. Leaving the convent was almost like getting a divorce. It wasn't an impulse move—I thought about it for five years before I actually left.

The world has changed a lot in the last seventeen years. I went into therapy to begin to catch up and figure things out. The most interesting thing I've discovered is that I'm not afraid of people anymore. I'm no longer that Irish farm girl who was afraid to make eye contact on the subway. I'm able to go out on dates and enjoy men's company. I'm more comfortable with myself. I'm still teaching, but I've left the Catholic school system and teach in public schools. I've opened my own Irish language school, and I find great personal satisfaction running my own business. I'm very excited about my future. I'm enjoying the music and dance of Ireland again, but I wouldn't want to go back to Ireland to live because I've gotten used to an American open-mindedness that only can exist in a country this large. I know I'm much more open-minded from living here. If I joined a convent in Ireland, I probably never would have left, but here the atmosphere is much more conducive to thought and change. I certainly would never have gone into therapy—that's a very American thing to do, to question and ask why. This is a wonderful country for the curious. I'm not just running on faith anymore. It's time for me to ask questions and find out who I am. I'm glad I had the courage to leave Ireland and then the convent. It makes me who I am today, and I'm enjoying getting to know myself better and I like who I am.